AND THE
DANGEROUS
BREAKFAST

ABOUT THE AUTHOR

KJARTAN POSKITT is the well-loved author of many hilarious books for children including Agatha Parrot and the Murderous Maths series, translated into over 30 languages. With a background in children's television, he is a tireless and brilliant performer.

ABOUT THE ILLUSTRATOR

PHILIP REEVE is an award-winning illustrator and author whose books have won the Carnegie, Guardian and Smarties Prizes.

Borgon the Axeboy

AND THE DANGEROUS BREAKFAST

Kjartan Poskitt

Illustrated by
Philip Reeve

ff

FABER & FABER

First published in 2014
by Faber and Faber Limited
Bloomsbury House
74–77 Great Russell Street
London WC1B 3DA

Designed by Faber
Printed and bound by CPI Group (UK) Ltd, Croydon CR4 0YY

A CIP record for this book is available from the British Library

978–0571–30733–3

2 4 6 8 10 9 7 5 3 1

To the real Uncle Jing,

who lives in Cumbria with his flying machine

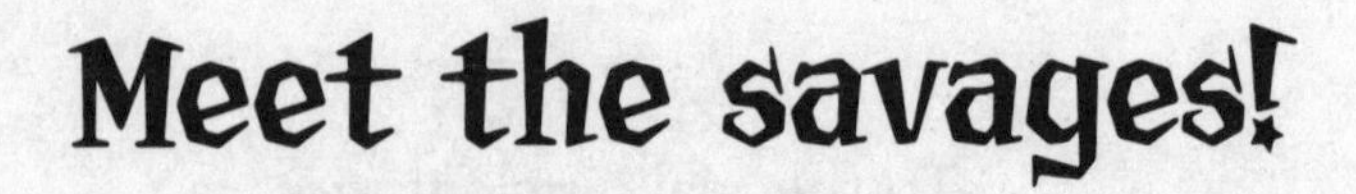

BORGON,
our hero!

Borgon's annoying
next-cave neighbour

FULGUT,
Borgon's dad
FULMA,
Borgon's mum
MUNGOID and HUNJAH, Borgon's pals

GOLGARTH BASIN

THE FIRE LANDS

RARGH!

HERE BE DRAGONS

THE PUNCH PIT

THE UPSIDE-DOWN MOUNTAINS

THE LOST DESERT

MOUNTAINS OF CHAOS

BOO-BA-DE-DOO
WAH OOOH
SHABBADA BE-BOO-BA DOOP
YEAH!

VALLEY OF THE SCAT CACTI

THE WANDERING JUNGLE

CONFUSED BUSH

N

THE LOST DESSERT

RUINED TEMPLE

Crocodile Tails

It was early morning in the Lost Desert. The vultures were snoozing in their nests, the scorpions were tucked up in their rock holes and even the rattlesnakes hadn't started to rattle. They were curled up underneath the cactuses, having lovely dreams about biting big animals and watching them fall over and die.

The sunlight broke over the mountains, and lit up a dusty patch of ground known as Golgarth Basin. The basin was surrounded by dark caves where all the different savages lived, and some strange noises were coming from one of them.

WAKKA-WAKKA CHOP CHOP SPLOTCH!

Borgon the Axeboy tucked his axe into his belt and hurried to the back of the cave, where his mum and dad were still asleep.

'Wake up!' he said. 'I've got a lovely surprise for you.'

'Eh? What?' came a sleepy voice.

'Come on! Get up! Come and see.'

Borgon's parents crawled out from underneath their mammoth-skin blanket. His mum was called Fulma. She was very tall, very skinny and had dark red spiky hair. Nobody else in the desert looked anything like her, especially not Borgon's dad. He was called Fulgut and he had a big head, a big nose, big arms, big ears . . . in fact everything about him was big.

Fulma and Fulgut were a special type of savage called barbarians. Barbarians were the toughest and scariest savages in the Lost Desert, but it didn't matter how tough and scary Borgon's mum and dad were supposed to be, they still got a shock when they saw what was waiting for them in the main part of the cave. The floor was covered with fresh bones and bits of green skin, and on the table was a huge dripping pile of raw meat.

'Borgon! What's this supposed to be?' asked Fulma.

'It's breakfast!' said Borgon proudly.

Fulma picked up a lump of meat. It was long and fat and still twitching.

'Borgon . . . this looks like a crocodile tail . . .' said Fulma.

'That's right!' said Borgon. 'You're always telling me that we're the last barbarians in the Lost Desert. We're supposed to be tougher and scarier than the other savages, so for once I've made us all a *real* barbarian breakfast.'

Fulma dropped the tail back on to the table.

SPLOTT!

'Sorry, Borgon,' she said. 'But I can't eat that.'

'Why?' asked Borgon. 'Isn't it lovely?'

'Yes, it's VERY lovely,' sighed Fulma.

'But I'm having my teeth sharpened today. I can't eat tough things like tails on teeth-sharpening day.'

'What?' gasped Borgon. 'After all my hard work?'

'Go on, dear,' said Fulgut. 'Have a try.'

Fulma picked up a tiny piece of loose meat. She tried to chew it but had to spit it out.

'It's no good,' she said. 'You and your dad will just have to eat it all between you.'

Borgon and Fulgut both did little bounces of joy. If there's one thing barbarians LOVE, it's having extra breakfast.

'**YARGHHHHHH!**' they cheered, then

they both opened their mouths and dived in, teeth first.

Fulma stood back and watched as the pile of tails started to disappear.

'It's a good breakfast, son,' said Fulgut with his mouth full. 'You're going to make a great barbarian one day.'

'But I'm a barbarian now!' said Borgon. 'I'm one of the maddest, baddest savages in the Lost Desert. **YARGHHHH!**'

Fulma shook her head. 'If you want to be a *real* barbarian, you need to be more like your father,' she said.

MUNCH SLOBBER BOILK CHOMP! agreed Fulgut.

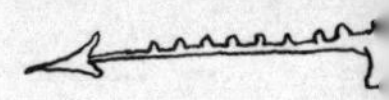

The old savage tipped back his big head and swallowed what was left of the tail in one big **GULP**. Then he gave off a whopping great **BURP**.

Fulma smiled. 'You see, Borgon? Now you try.'

Borgon grabbed another crocodile tail. It was as big as his own leg, so he picked up a long rusty dagger and started to cut off a slice.

Fulma shook her head.

'NO NO NO!' she said. 'You're not a baby any more. If you need to cut it, use your axe!'

'Even when we're sitting at the table?' said Borgon.

'Absolutely!' grinned Fulgut. 'That's what your Uncle Jing always did, and he was the maddest barbarian ever.'

Borgon leaped to his feet excitedly. He pulled his axe from his belt, raised it high above his head, then whacked it down into the crocodile tail as hard as he could.

SPLUTCH!

'Well done,' laughed Fulgut. 'An axe always turns a meal into a party.'

Borgon chewed away on a lump of tail.

GOBBLE BLONCH SLOOP!

'That's it!' said Fulgut. 'Barbarians always eat loudly. It makes all the other savages jealous.'

'Don't forget to burp . . .' said Fulma.

BURP! went Borgon.

'. . . and wipe your hands on your hair.'

'Or better still,' said Fulgut, 'wipe your hands on somebody else's hair! That's what I always used to do.'

'Didn't anyone complain?' asked Borgon.

'No one dared!' laughed Fulma. 'Your dad was the fiercest savage the Lost Desert has ever known.'

The old savage smiled, then did a big yawn.

'That was a long time ago,' admitted Fulgut. 'That was when your mum was the SCARIEST savage the Lost Desert has ever known. They used to call her Freaky Fulma.'

'Dad, did you ever wipe your hands on Mum's hair?' asked Borgon.

Oh dear! Fulma did NOT think that was funny. She hissed through her teeth, her eyes narrowed to tiny slits and her dark red hair stuck out even more.

'We don't talk about that,' said Fulgut hurriedly.

'It must have been great being you two in the old days,' sighed Borgon. 'What about that time when you ambushed the Evil Snake People and tied all their tails together? Or when you went tightrope walking over that volcano crater? And, Dad, is it true you once drove off a whole gang of wild desert bandits with a teaspoon?'

'It's not quite true,' chuckled Fulgut.

'He had a fork as well,' said Fulma.

'It served them right for trying to attack me at dinner time,' said Fulgut.

'Lucky you,' said Borgon. 'Barbarians used

to have loads of fights and excitement, but I don't. All I ever get to do is eat and burp.'

'Don't give up hope, son,' said Fulgut. 'You never know when something extremely nasty and ridiculously dangerous might crop up.'

'Right, you two, I'm off,' said Fulma. She went over to the mouth of the cave and gave a sharp whistle. A dark red horse trotted across the sandy basin to meet her. (That's right, Fulma had dark red hair and also a dark red horse. Matching hair and horse was the top fashion for lady savages.)

'But, Mum! You haven't had any of the breakfast I made,' said Borgon.

‘I know,’ said Fulma. ‘But like I said, I can’t eat tails right now. I’ll have to get something when I’m back.’

And with that, Fulgut lifted her up on to her horse and she galloped away.

Fun and Danger

There was only one crocodile tail left on the table.

'Shall we save it for Mum to have later?' asked Borgon.

'She won't want it,' said Fulgut. 'Why don't you make her something else?'

'But I want to make her a real barbarian

breakfast, Dad,' said Borgon.

'That's easy enough,' chuckled Fulgut. 'Anything can be a barbarian breakfast. It just needs two special ingredients.'

'Like what?'

'It's got to be FUN and it's got to be DANGEROUS.'

Borgon grinned. He liked the sound of that!

'Go on then, Dad,' he said. 'Give me some ideas.'

'Well, your Uncle Jing used to make rattlesnake pie,' said Fulgut.

'With live rattlesnakes?' said Borgon.

'Of course!' said Fulgut. 'Otherwise

where's the fun? He did a really nice roast elephant too.'

'Roast elephant?' said Borgon. 'Why was that dangerous?'

'The elephant didn't want to get in the oven,' laughed Fulgut. 'It went crazy!'

Borgon's eyes were popping with excitement. 'That must have been the most dangerous breakfast ever!'

'Not quite,' said Fulgut. 'I made a special breakfast to celebrate the first time your mum had her teeth sharpened. Now *that* was really dangerous.'

'Wow!' said Borgon excitedly. 'What was it?'

'I'm not telling you,' said Fulgut. 'It was far too dangerous.'

'Oh, Dad!' moaned Borgon. 'We're supposed to be barbarians! There's no such thing as TOO dangerous.'

'Oh yes there is,' said Fulgut.

'No there isn't!' said Borgon. 'So tell me.'

Fulgut checked to see that no one was listening, then he bent down to whisper in Borgon's ear.

Borgon's jaw dropped open in amazement. 'Wow, Dad!' he said. 'Is that true? Did you really make that for Mum's breakfast?'

'Yes,' nodded Fulgut proudly. 'It was the Best Barbarian Breakfast Ever, and your mum LOVED it.'

'Then I'm going to make it too,' said Borgon. 'I'm a barbarian, and Mum said I should be more like you!'

'No no NO!' said Fulgut, but it was too late.

Borgon was already charging around the

cave. He grabbed a triple-headed spear, a mighty sword, a battle mallet, a steel net, his axe and a whole bag of extra bits.

'Don't do this, Borgon!' pleaded Fulgut. 'Your mum will go mad if she finds out I told you about that breakfast.'

'Then don't tell her,' said Borgon. 'Besides, I want it to be a nice surprise for her.'

'But you could end up DEAD,' said Fulgut. 'What do I say to her then?'

'That's your problem!' laughed Borgon. 'Because if I'm dead I won't be here, will I? I'll be in heaven with all the barbarian gods and Uncle Jing. **YARGHHHH!**'

Tomatoes, Stones and Scorpions

Borgon ran outside to his horse, clutching all his weapons. He leaped up with a mighty leap, but the horse stepped forwards with a mighty step so Borgon hit the ground with a mighty **CRUNCH!**

'Hey, Borgon!' shouted a cheeky voice. 'You're supposed to sit ON the horse, not underneath it!'

Borgon groaned. It was Grizzy, the nosey girl who lived over on the far side of Golgarth Basin. She was sitting outside her cave, eating her own breakfast out of a bowl.

'**GRRRR!**' growled Borgon and he waved his axe.

Grizzy just pulled a face and giggled.

Borgon stamped his foot crossly. Grizzy never treated him with any respect. It wasn't right. Grizzy was supposed to be SCARED of him! After all, he wasn't just a normal boring savage like she was. He was a barbarian.

'HEY, EVERYBODY!' shouted Grizzy. 'Borgon's forgotten how to get on a horse. Ha ha ha!'

By this time two other savages had come out to see what was going on, but if Grizzy thought they were going to laugh, she was wrong. Mungoid and Hunjah were

Borgon's best friends. Mungoid went to help Borgon up while Hunjah held the horse.

'What are you up to, Borgon?' asked Mungoid, who was big and chunky, with a head like a brick.

'I'm going to make the Best Barbarian Breakfast Ever,' said Borgon.

'Looks like it's going to be fun!' said Mungoid. He picked up the axe and tossed it over to the young barbarian.

'Of course it's going to be fun!' cheered Borgon. He swished the axe around his head a few times. '**YARGHHHH!**'

'Why do you need all those weapons? Can't you just use a spoon?' asked Hunjah.

Hunjah was the skinny one who always wore a big straw hat because his mum told him to.

'Because this breakfast is DANGEROUS!' said Borgon. 'In fact, it's so dangerous, the only person who has ever made it before is my dad.'

'Big deal!' said Grizzy. 'The nearest thing you barbarians get to danger is tripping over your own shadows.'

'You wouldn't say that if you knew what I was making,' said Borgon.

'So what are you making?' asked Grizzy.

'It's a secret,' said Borgon. 'All you need to know is that it's the most dangerous breakfast ever.'

Grizzy scowled, and the others laughed. If there was one thing Grizzy HATED, it was secrets that she didn't know.

'Ha ha!' laughed Hunjah. 'We know a secret and you don't. Ha ha!'

'Actually . . . we don't know either,' said Mungoid.

'Oh,' said Hunjah, and he stopped laughing.

Grizzy picked up Borgon's bag of extra bits which had landed at her feet.

'So what's in here?' she asked.

'Give me that!' said Borgon, and he snatched it from her before she could look inside.

'Oooh!' said Grizzy. 'You're a bit touchy today.'

'It's all part of the secret,' replied Borgon.

'You don't fool me,' said Grizzy. 'I bet my breakfast is a whole load more dangerous than yours. Look!' She showed them her bowl. It was full of grey lumpy stuff with black spiky bits sticking out of it. 'Scorpion porridge,' she said.

She stuck her spoon in and gulped down a big mouthful. The boys all looked horrified.

'What's the matter?' grinned Grizzy. 'Are you scared of a few scorpions?'

'Scorpions are fine,' said Mungoid. 'But porridge?'

'**BLURGH!**' laughed the boys, pretending to be sick.

'Your breakfast isn't dangerous, Grizzy, it's just gross,' said Borgon.

'So what's a dangerous breakfast, then?' asked Grizzy crossly.

'I once had a tomato without washing it first,' said Hunjah.

'HA HA HA!' laughed the others. Although Hunjah was their friend, he really was the most pathetic savage in the Lost Desert.

'Well, you're braver than me,' said Mungoid. 'I daren't eat tomatoes at all.'

'Why not?' asked Grizzy.

'Soft food's too dangerous!' said the chunky savage. 'My mouth gets confused. I end up chewing my own tongue.'

'Then what do you eat?' asked Grizzy.

Mungoid reached into a pouch hanging from his belt and pulled out a handful of coloured pebbles. 'These,' he said. 'Do you want one?'

'They're stones, you weirdo!' said Grizzy, pulling a face.

'They're not just any old stones,' explained Mungoid. 'These ones are pink marble.'

He popped one of the pebbles into his mouth and bit down on it with his huge teeth.

CERR-ACK!

Mungoid smiled happily as he crunched away.

'Hey, Borgon!' said Hunjah, suddenly sounding worried. 'Can you hurry up and go?'

Borgon saw that his horse was merrily chewing away at Hunjah's big straw hat. 'Hold him steady! Here I come!'

He leaped up on to his horse, then steered it around to face the open desert.

'Are you sure you can't tell us anything about this breakfast?' asked Mungoid.

'Sorry,' said Borgon. 'I want it to be a surprise for my mum.'

'OK,' said Mungoid. 'But you have to promise you'll tell us about it when you get back.'

'No,' said Borgon. 'I'll tell you IF I get back!'

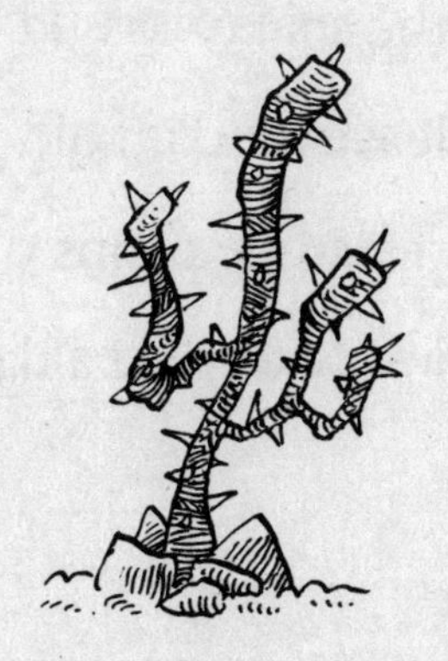

The Fire Lands

It was the middle of the morning and the desert rocks were starting to creak in the heat of the sun. The vultures circled overhead, the snakes hissed from underneath the cactus leaves and an old yak collapsed and died on the stone plains of the Lost Desert. It was a lovely day for a dangerous adventure.

There was just one little thing spoiling it. As Borgon rode along, he heard a little clip-clopping noise behind him. He pretended that he couldn't hear it. With any luck the clip-clopping noise would give up and turn back, leaving him to go on alone.

Eventually, Borgon reached an old wooden sign where the path divided into two. The sign had an arrow at one end and some squiggles drawn on it, but Borgon had no idea what it meant. He scratched his head in confusion. He wanted to go to the Fire Lands where all the nastiest creatures in the Lost Desert lived, but which way was it?

'Ha ha ha!' laughed a voice behind him.

'You barbarians are pathetic. Ha ha ha!'

Borgon swung round to face Grizzy who had been following him all the way on her little grey horse.

'GO HOME!' he shouted.

'You can't make me,' said Grizzy. 'Besides,

I've come to see this barbarian breakfast.'

'But it's too dangerous for ordinary savages like you! Did you tell your mum you were coming?'

'I didn't bother,' said Grizzy. 'Because I know it won't be dangerous at all.'

'Well that's where you're *wrong*. Do you have any idea where I'm going to get this breakfast?' he asked.

'Yes,' nodded Grizzy. 'You're going to find a dragon.'

'What?' gasped Borgon. 'How could you possibly know that?'

'The sign,' said Grizzy. 'It says *To the Dragons*.'

Borgon stared at Grizzy in astonishment. 'Then why aren't you scared?' he asked. 'Why aren't you riding off screaming in terror?'

'Because you might need some help,' said Grizzy. 'And if we're dealing with dragons, I've got just the thing.'

Grizzy reached into her pocket and pulled out a little flappy thing and waved it at him. Borgon immediately ducked, thinking it was going to fire some poisoned darts or something, but it didn't. It just flapped.

'Is that all it does?' he said. 'It's the most pathetic weapon I've ever seen.'

'It's not a weapon, you clot,' said Grizzy. 'It's the *Book of All Things*, and it tells you everything about everything, including dragons. You should learn to read.'

'Pah!' sniffed Borgon. 'I'm a barbarian. We ride and fight and shout **YARGHHHH**. Why would I need to read?'

'Then you could understand that sign for a start,' said Grizzy. 'It's telling you which path leads to the dragons.'

'Barbarians don't need signs!' retorted Borgon. 'I'll find a dragon with my awesome tracking powers.'

Borgon leaned right down from the top of his horse until his nose almost touched the ground. 'Aha! This path has got a bent blade of grass and two overturned pebbles. A dragon definitely went up there!'

'Oh yeah?' said Grizzy, then she set off

down the other path.

'Where are you going?' Borgon shouted after her.

'To the dragons,' said Grizzy. 'The sign says they're this way.'

'But what about the pebbles?' protested Borgon. 'And the bent grass . . . ?'

'You've got it wrong,' said Grizzy. 'It's *this* way. So are you coming, or are you scared?'

The Smoking Tree

Borgon and Grizzy rode in silence. It was partly because they wanted to catch the dragons by surprise, but mainly because Borgon was having a HUGE sulk. Poor Borgon! He was very proud of his tracking powers, but he'd been made to look silly by a little wooden sign.

The horses were heading down into a dark wooded valley, when Grizzy noticed a big black patch on one of the trees. She went over and poked it. Her finger came away covered in sticky black soot.

'It's a burn mark!' said Grizzy. 'It could be from a dragon.'

'I still say that a dragon went down the other path,' growled Borgon.

'But you didn't find one,' said Grizzy. 'And the sign says the dragons are this way, and this tree has definitely been burnt by something.'

The path got darker and darker as it twisted through the woods. More and more trees were covered in black burn marks, which made Borgon get sulkier and sulkier.

'Cheer up, Borgon,' said Grizzy. 'It doesn't matter.'

'What doesn't matter?'

'You being wrong.'

'I am not wrong!' bellowed Borgon. 'I bet there hasn't been a dragon down here for years. This is a waste of time.'

Just as he said that, their horses came to a stop next to a tree that was still smoking.

'There MUST be a dragon round here

somewhere,' said Grizzy.

'No there isn't!' said Borgon.

'Roar,' said a dragon politely as he watched them from behind a firethorn bush. He was quite a shy dragon and didn't like the look of the two savages, so he was gently warning them off.

Borgon and Grizzy stared into the darkness.

'I think there's something in there,' said Grizzy, trying to sound casual. 'Maybe it's a dragon?'

'No it's not,' snapped Borgon.

'ROAR,' said the dragon a bit louder.

'It sounds pretty close,' said Grizzy. 'And it's dark here. Shall we move on a bit?'

'Why?' said Borgon. 'That's not a dragon.'

'ROAAARRGH!' said the dragon even louder.

'And that's not a dragon either,' said Borgon. 'I'm not going anywhere until you admit I'm right.'

'OK,' said Grizzy. 'You're right. Of course you're right. You're very, very right. That was not a dragon.'

'Thank you,' said Borgon triumphantly.

ROAAARRRRGGHHHH!

'Actually,' said Borgon, 'now I come to think of it, that *might* be a dragon.'

'**YARGHHHH!**' they both screamed.

The two horses leaped over the burning tree and off they went.

GALLOPY-CLIPPETY-CLOPPETY-WHIZZ!

The Little Lizard

The two savages charged through the blackened trees and smoky bushes until they came to a small clearing.

Borgon clattered down from his horse then quickly unrolled the steel net and hung it between two trees to make a dragon trap. Meanwhile Grizzy sat herself down and looked through the *Book of All Things*.

'Have you ever seen a dragon before?' asked Grizzy.

'No,' admitted Borgon.

'The book says you can always recognise a dragon by its orange eyes,' said Grizzy.

'Who cares what your silly book says?' laughed Borgon. 'All we need to know is that dragons are BIG and they BLAST FIRE.'

'Please yourself,' said Grizzy. 'There are loads of dragon recipes in here too. What are you making?'

'I'm not telling you,' said Borgon.

'How about dragon soup?' suggested Grizzy. 'Oh, actually you can't make that.'

'Why not?' asked Borgon.

'Because you need two onions and a jug of cream,' said Grizzy. 'And you haven't got those with you . . . unless they're in that bag?'

Grizzy pointed at the bag of extra bits that was still hanging from Borgon's horse.

'That bag is none of your business,' said Borgon. 'Now stop talking. I need to listen out for this dragon.'

So Grizzy stopped talking and Borgon waited by the net, clutching his axe. He stared into the darkness of the trees, ready to pounce. But everything was silent – until Grizzy turned a page in her book.

'Oooh!' said Grizzy. 'How about dragon burgers? Perfect for parties.'

'Shh!' said Borgon.

'Or there's dragon pie,' said Grizzy. 'I can do the pastry if you like.'

'Oh, give up, Grizzy!' said Borgon. 'The Best Barbarian Breakfast Ever won't be in your silly little book.'

'Why not?' said Grizzy.

'Because it's far too dangerous,' said Borgon. 'My dad even tried to stop me making it. Now be quiet.'

Everything went silent again.

'Ha ha ha!' laughed Grizzy.

'QUIET!' whispered Borgon.

'Oh, but you've got to hear this,' said Grizzy. 'Did you know there's a recipe for dragon toenail custard?'

Borgon stomped over to Grizzy and pulled the book from her hands.

'This isn't a game,' he said. 'If this dragon creeps up on us while you're talking, then we could be fried alive!'

'Maybe,' said Grizzy. 'But you have to admit, dragon toenail custard is funny.'

'No it's not,' said Borgon, and he stomped back to his net.

Grizzy tucked her book into her pocket and decided to pick some flowers. Borgon carried on waiting for the dragon. And waiting . . . And waiting.

Eventually Grizzy came over.

'Pssst!' she whispered.

Borgon tried to ignore her.

'Pssst!' she whispered again. 'Can you hear me?'

'No,' said Borgon.

'Yes you can,' said Grizzy.

'What do you want now?' snapped Borgon.

'Is this dragon coming?' said Grizzy. 'Because I'm getting bored. Are you getting bored?'

'No.'

'Well, I am,' said Grizzy. 'You wait here. I'll go and see where it's got to.'

'No, hang on!' said Borgon. 'You can't just go looking for a dragon.'

'Why not?'

'Because it's a dragon!' said Borgon. 'You should be scared silly!'

'Well of course I'm scared,' admitted Grizzy. 'But I'd rather be scared than bored.'

Borgon watched in horror as the girl skipped off into the trees armed with nothing more than a little bunch of flowers.

'Come back,' Borgon called after her. 'You haven't got any weapons!'

'I've got *one*,' shouted Grizzy's voice.

'What?' said Borgon.

Weee – donk!

A stone flew out of the trees and hit Borgon on the nose.

'Ha ha ha!' laughed Grizzy.

'**GRRR!**' growled Borgon.

It was SO unfair. Why was Grizzy having more fun than he was? What's more, if anything happened to her, Borgon knew that somehow he'd be the one in trouble. He had to go after her, but there was no time to collect up the horses and the big weapons. He ran into the woods clutching his axe.

It wasn't hard to follow Grizzy's trail. She had picked every flower along the way, leaving just the empty flower stalks.

Borgon finally spotted her sitting on a little rock surrounded by big floppy mushrooms. Grizzy had caught a fat spider by the leg, and was dangling it in front of a little yellow lizard that was sitting on the biggest and floppiest mushroom.

'Come on, eat up!' she said.

'What are you doing?' asked Borgon. 'You're supposed to be watching out for dragons.'

'But he's hungry!' said Grizzy.

Borgon watched as the lizard's tongue flicked out and lapped up the spider. A big smile appeared on his face.

'Hey, Grizzy, you've just given me a great idea! We could use that lizard thing for bait.'

'What do you mean?'

'We tie the lizard to the net, and then when the dragon comes to eat it, we trap him!'

'That's mean!' said Grizzy, scooping up the little yellow lizard. 'You can't do that.'

'Oh yes I can,' said Borgon. 'Give him to me!'

'No, go away,' said Grizzy.

Borgon pulled his axe from his belt and took a step towards her. 'Come on, Grizzy, don't be—'

ROAARRRRRGGHHHH!

A massive flame cloud shot from the little lizard's mouth. Borgon's axe crashed to the ground and lay there with the red-hot blade sizzling in the undergrowth. The thunderous roar echoed through the trees, then it shot up the path and turned right at the wooden sign before bouncing all the way back to Golgarth Basin where Mungoid and Hunjah were feeding the ostriches.

'What was that?' asked Hunjah.

'It sounded like Borgon making his dangerous breakfast!' said Mungoid.

A Big Fat Lie

For a few moments it was silent. Borgon and Grizzy lay curled up on the ground with their hands clasped over their ears. Eventually Borgon raised his head. The little lizard had hopped back on to his mushroom.

'What IS that?' asked Borgon admiringly.

'Do you think it's a dragon?' said Grizzy.

'That little thing?' Borgon shook his head. 'It *can't* be.'

'I can soon check,' said Grizzy. She flicked through her book and then stared at the lizard again. 'Be honest. What colour would you say its eyes are?'

'Orange,' said Borgon.

'Then it *is* a dragon!' said Grizzy, snapping the book shut.

'But it's tiny,' said Borgon. 'My dad said dragons are huge!'

'Maybe your dad wanted to sound tough, so he told you he made breakfast from a giant dragon,' said Grizzy.

'My dad doesn't make stuff up,' said Borgon.

'Oh no?' giggled Grizzy, pointing at the dragon. 'Look at it! No wonder he tried to stop you coming out here. He didn't want you to know the truth about the tiny dragons! HA HA HA HA HA! Your dad told you a big fat lie!'

Grizzy rolled around laughing, thumping the ground with her fists and wiping the tears out of her eyes.

'Don't you dare laugh at my dad!' growled Borgon. 'He is the fiercest barbarian the desert has ever known.'

'Oh yeah?' said Grizzy. 'Then what was it about this breakfast he made that was SO dangerous?'

'It's a secret,' said Borgon.

'No it isn't,' said Grizzy. 'There's only one thing it can be. It's a teeny weeny little dragon sausage!'

'No it is NOT,' said Borgon.

'Well, whatever it is, I'm not going to let

you hurt my new friend,' said Grizzy.

And before Borgon could stop her, Grizzy had crawled over to the dragon and picked him up again.

'Put it back right now!' hissed Borgon.

'Calm down!' said Grizzy, stroking the little yellow head with her finger. 'Don't wet your barbarian pants.'

'But if you get yourself blasted, I'll be the one in trouble.'

'I'm perfectly safe,' said Grizzy. 'You're the one that upset him. He likes me. Aw, look, he's licking my hand! He is just SO cute, aren't you, my little baby draggy yum yums?'

'Baby draggy yum yums?' repeated

Borgon. 'Look what he did to my axe!'

Borgon went over to his weapon. The handle was still hot, so he picked it up with his fingertips, leaving a black axe-shaped burn mark on the ground.

'Aw!' said Grizzy. 'Poor little Borgon. Diddums little Barbarian axe get too hot for your little handy pandy?'

Borgon raised his axe in the air.

'I'm warning you, Grizzy,' he said. 'I came here with a job to do. Now pass that dragon over.'

Grizzy carefully put the dragon back on his mushroom.

'OK,' said Grizzy. 'If you want him, then

you come and get him . . . IF you think you're tough enough.'

Grizzy moved back out of the way.

Borgon took a step forwards.

The dragon opened his mouth and a wisp of smoke came out. It was a warning! Borgon quickly stepped back again. Keeping his distance, Borgon circled around the mushroom to try and sneak up from behind, but the little dragon wasn't silly. It twizzled itself round to watch him.

'Well, go on, then,' said Grizzy. 'Give it your best shot. I'll sweep up your bones and take them back to your dad.'

Borgon had no choice. He raised his axe in the air with one hand, and got his other hand ready to grab the dragon. He took a deep breath, then closed his eyes and braced himself for a scorching blast of white-hot flame.

'**YARGHHHH!**' he shouted and charged forwards.

ROAARRGHHHH!

'YOW!' screamed Borgon. 'YOW YOW ow ow oooooh . . . eh?'

For some reason, it wasn't hurting. Borgon decided he must already be dead. He just stood there and waited for some angels to take him up to barbarian heaven so he could meet up with his mad Uncle Jing and eat live rattlesnake pie.

'That was boring,' said Grizzy.

When Borgon realised that he wasn't dead after all, he opened

his eyes. The little dragon was sitting on the mushroom, looking up at him sweetly.

'What happened?' asked Grizzy.

'He must have run out of fire,' said Borgon.

Grizzy came over and gave the little creature a stroke. The dragon licked her hand and then rolled over to have its silver tummy tickled.

'He's got a tiny flame coming out of his nose,' said Grizzy.

The dragon was happily wriggling and twisting under Grizzy's fingers when suddenly . . .

Kee-chiff!

The dragon sneezed. The last flicker of flame shot out and sizzled the edge of the mushroom.

Grizzy stood up and sighed.

'All right, Borgon, you win,' she said sadly. 'If he can't defend himself, then I suppose you can do what you like.'

'No I can't,' said Borgon. He tucked his axe into his belt, then reached down to give the dragon a friendly tickle. 'How can I make a dangerous barbarian breakfast without any danger?'

'Stop moaning,' said Grizzy. 'You came to get a dragon and you've got one. You should be pleased.'

'But it's all gone wrong,' sighed Borgon sadly. 'I'm a barbarian! I wanted to meet up with a BIG dragon. I wanted to attack it while it blasted me with flames. I'm Borgon the Axeboy, not Borgon the tummy tickler!'

Borgon gave the dragon a final stroke then stood up. The dragon flipped back on to his feet and Borgon gave him a little wave.

'Goodbye, my little friend,' he said. 'I hope

you get your fire back soon.'

'So what happens now?' asked Grizzy, as they returned to the horses.

'I'm going home,' said Borgon.

'What a waste of a morning,' said Grizzy, trudging along behind him. 'I wanted to see a bit of danger.'

'Really? Then you're going to enjoy this afternoon,' said Borgon.

'Why?'

'Because I'm going to ask my dad why he lied to me. And that's when it's going to get REALLY dangerous.'

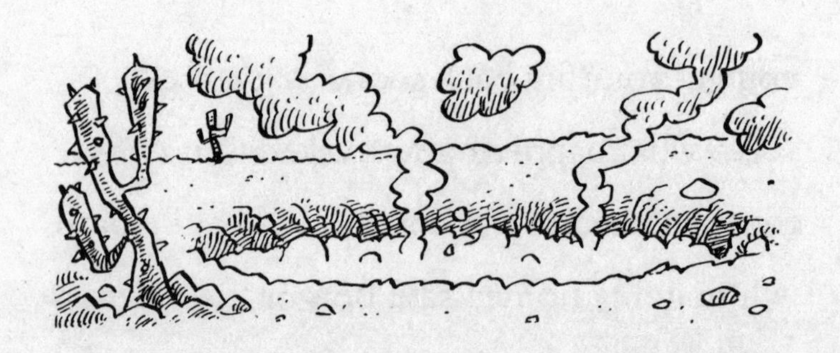

The Punch Pit

By the time Borgon and Grizzy got back to the signpost, the sun was directly overhead. The horses were hot and tired, so they got down, and let the animals wander off to find a bit of shade.

Grizzy was grumpy because she'd left her bunch of flowers somewhere, but that wasn't important. Borgon was grumpy because he was going home without a dangerous breakfast. He looked up the path where he'd first seen the bent blade of grass and two overturned pebbles.

'I STILL say a dragon went that way,' said Borgon sulkily.

'Then you're still wrong,' said Grizzy. 'And anyway, why would a dragon go that way? The sign says it goes to something called the Punch Pit.'

'The Punch Pit?' repeated Borgon. 'I've always wondered where that was. Dad refused to tell me.'

'I'm not surprised,' said Grizzy, who was

already looking it up in the *Book of All Things*. 'According to this, it's a purple lake made out of mouldy fruit.'

'And it STINKS!' grinned Borgon.

'My book doesn't say that,' said Grizzy.

'No, but my dad did,' said Borgon. 'He said it's got dirty great bubbles that come up and when they pop, the smell could knock over a hippopotamus.'

'I don't believe that,' said Grizzy. 'I bet it's another one of his big fat lies.'

'No it's not!' said Borgon crossly. 'He went there with Uncle Jing. And you'll never guess what they did.'

'What?'

'They drank it.'

'Oh,' said Grizzy. 'Well, I do believe that. It's just the sort of stupid thing barbarians would do.'

'IT WAS NOT STUPID!' shouted Borgon. 'Oh, well, actually it *was* pretty stupid,' he admitted. 'Dad said it was so gassy that Uncle Jing blew the backside off his trousers. HA HA HA!'

Grizzy wrinkled her nose in disgust.

'Oh, come on!' said Borgon. 'Don't you think that's funny?'

'No, it's just pathetic, and barbarians are pathetic,' said Grizzy. 'In fact, if there's one thing I've found out today, it's just how totally pathetic barbarians are.'

Grizzy saw Borgon's eyes going red. He drew his axe then charged at her.

'**YARGHHHH!**' screamed the Axeboy.

'NO!' screamed Grizzy. She had never seen him like this before. Surely Borgon wasn't going to chop her to bits just because she said barbarians were pathetic?

Here Comes Mummy!

A large black shadow covered them both. With a **crunch** and a **splurt** Borgon drove his axe upwards into the belly of the swooping dragon. The giant beast gurgled horribly. Its wings flapped and its legs thrashed but it couldn't stop itself hitting the ground and skidding along helplessly until it came up against some rocks.

BLUMP FLUMP BLATTER!

Grizzy ran off and dived for cover behind a fat cactus, but where had Borgon got to?

The dragon staggered to its feet. It was as big as ten horses, with bulging eyes and a long arrow-headed tail. As it gasped for breath, long flames spluttered from its mouth and blasts of sparks and dirty smoke exploded from its nostrils. Black blood was dripping out of its belly and splashing into a thick pool on the ground. In the middle of the pool was a crumpled barbarian-shaped heap.

The heap wasn't moving so Grizzy picked up a small stone and threw it. The stone curled up through the air, soared over the dragon's tail and then came down and smacked Borgon right on the nose.

'YEOWW!' yelped Borgon as he woke up.

While the dragon was looking the other way, Grizzy ran out and dragged Borgon back to hide behind the cactus with her.

'Well?' said Borgon triumphantly. 'Well? WELL?'

'Well what?' asked Grizzy.

'I was right, wasn't I?' said Borgon. 'A dragon DID go up there. And it was BIG, so my dad did NOT lie!'

'Yes, OK, you were right,' admitted Grizzy. 'But why was that other dragon so small?'

'It must have been a baby,' said Borgon.

'This is the one we came for!'

The two of them peered out from behind the cactus. The dragon was trying to make its way back up the path. It flapped its wings, but then fell forwards and smacked its head on the ground. **FUBBLUMP**. The great beast lay there grunting and panting and thrashing its tail around crossly.

'Quick!' said Grizzy. 'Let's go while it isn't looking.'

'Go where?' asked Borgon.

'Home!' said Grizzy.

'You go home if you want to,' said Borgon, stepping out from behind the cactus. 'I've got a breakfast to make.'

Borgon's axe was still lying in the pool of black blood. He went to get it but Grizzy dashed ahead of him. She snatched up the axe and raised it over her head.

'Stop right there!' warned Grizzy.

'What are you doing?' asked Borgon.

'You've already hurt that dragon enough,' said Grizzy.

'Well, pardon me,' said Borgon. 'I was only saving your life.'

'Get back,' said Grizzy.

Borgon took a step backwards, but only because the axe was heavier than Grizzy had expected and she was starting to wobble a bit. There were many brave and heroic ways a barbarian could die, but being accidentally chopped in half by a wobbly girl savage with an axe wasn't one of them.

'Give me that before you hurt yourself,' said Borgon.

'NO!' said Grizzy. 'You can't have it.'

'Please yourself,' said Borgon. 'I need to get something from my horse.'

Borgon set off, but Grizzy shot past him and got to the horses first. She grabbed the triple-headed spear and pointed it at Borgon, still holding his axe in the air with the other hand.

'I'm not letting you have this either,' she said.

'I don't want it,' said Borgon.

'And you can't have this . . . or this!'

Grizzy grabbed the mighty sword and

the battle mallet, and tried to hold them all steady and point them at Borgon and look frightening at the same time.

Wobble wobble wobble.

'What's the matter with you?' asked Borgon.

'That might be a mummy dragon,' cried Grizzy desperately. 'And the little dragon that we saw might be her baby sitting on a mushroom waiting for her to come back. So you CAN'T just kill it for breakfast. I won't let you.'

'Whatever you say.' Borgon smiled. 'You can have all the weapons if it makes you happy. All I want is the bag.'

Grizzy had forgotten about the bag hanging from Borgon's horse.

'No sudden movements,' said Grizzy. 'I mean it!'

Borgon went over to the bag and reached inside. Grizzy raised all the weapons in the air, ready to attack him with everything at once if she had to.

'I wanted this to be a secret,' said Borgon. 'But I suppose you had to find out some time.'

Very slowly, Borgon pulled something out of the bag. Grizzy was so astonished, she dropped all the weapons to the ground with a big **CLUNK!**

‘What have you got there?’ said Grizzy suspiciously.

‘It’s a slice of bread,’ said Borgon.

‘Bread?’ gasped Grizzy. ‘Is that how your dad killed a dragon?’

Borgon shook his head and laughed. ‘He didn’t *kill* a dragon. That would have been far too easy. Dragons are a lot more DANGEROUS when they’re alive . . . and more FUN too!’

'Then I don't get it,' Grizzy said, looking very confused. 'What breakfast can you make with a live dragon and a slice of bread?'

'The Best Barbarian Breakfast Ever!' chuckled Borgon.

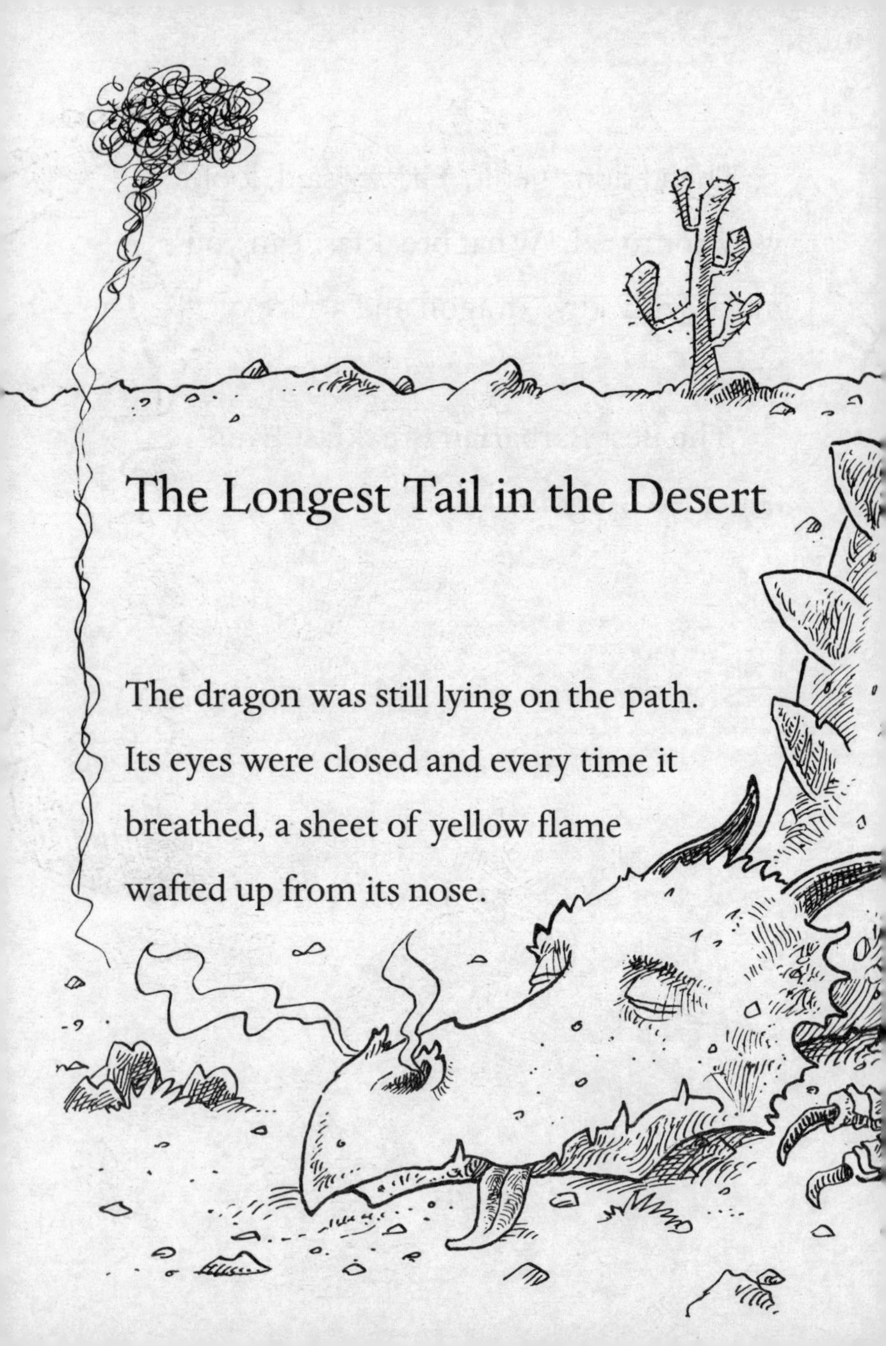

The Longest Tail in the Desert

The dragon was still lying on the path. Its eyes were closed and every time it breathed, a sheet of yellow flame wafted up from its nose.

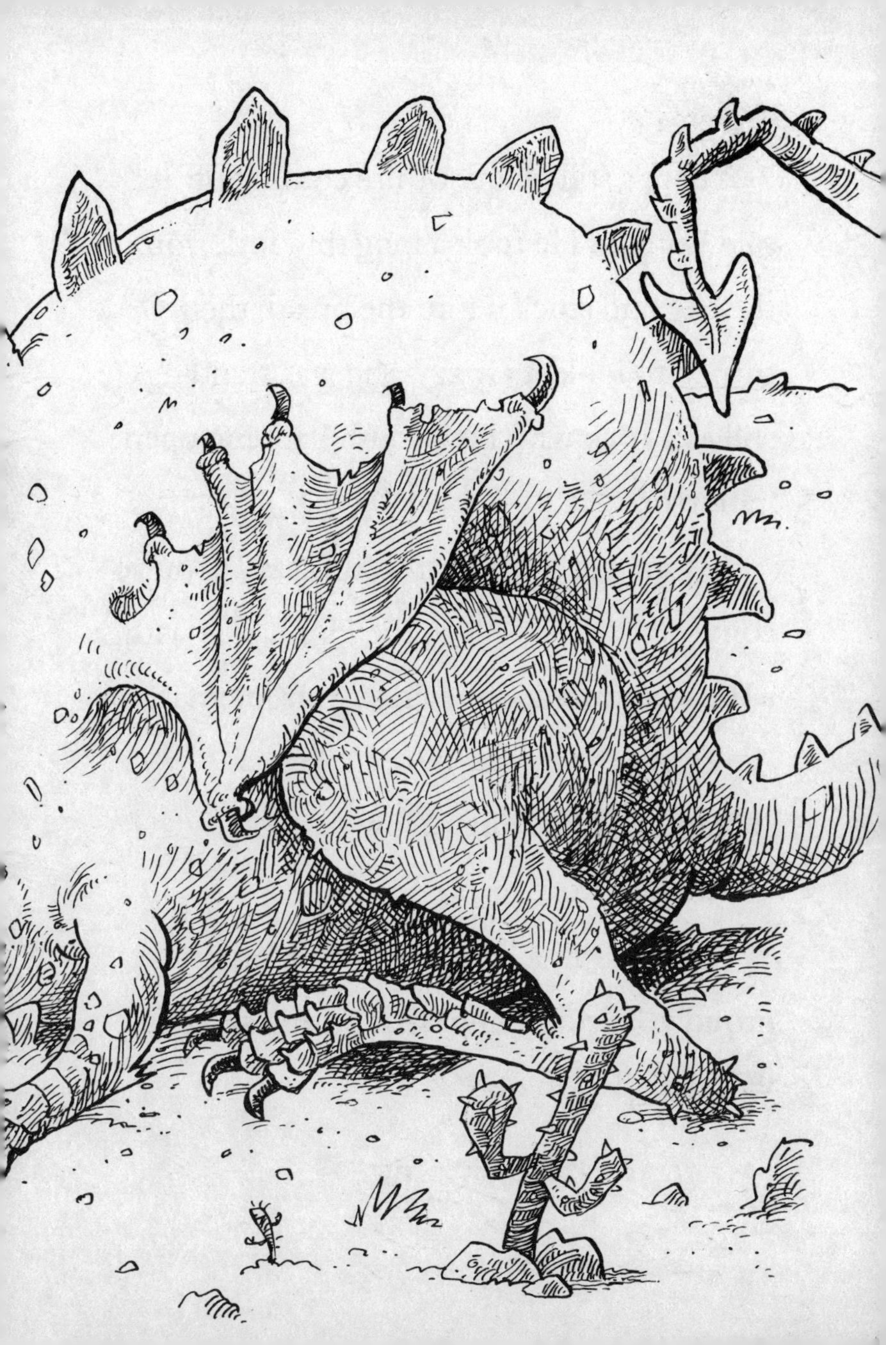

'There's still plenty of fire coming off it,' said Borgon. He took a long thin fork from the bag and stuck it into the bread, then turned to look at Grizzy. She was standing still as a rock with her mouth hanging open in horror.

'Let me get this right,' said Grizzy. 'You've come all the way out to the Fire Lands with a horse and weapons to risk your life making . . . TOAST?'

'Yup,' said Borgon.

'Why?'

'Because I'm a barbarian,' said Borgon proudly. 'We do things that boring savages wouldn't dream of.'

He swished the fork around a few times to make sure the bread wasn't going to fall off. 'Right then, here I go,' he said.

As Borgon set off towards the dragon, Grizzy realised she would feel very strange if she had to ride back on her own, especially with Borgon's empty horse trotting along beside her. What would Mungoid and Hunjah say? What would Borgon's dad say? Worst of all, what would Freaky Fulma say?

'Hang on!' cried Grizzy. 'You can't just walk up to a dragon and stick a bit of bread in its face.'

'Why not?' said Borgon.

'You saw what the baby dragon did. This giant could roast a whole herd of elephants with one blast!'

'**YARGHHHH!**' said Borgon. 'If my dad did it, then so can I.'

'But he's a big fat ugly savage,' said Grizzy. 'And you're just a small fat ugly savage.'

The dragon did a sleepy grunt.

GRORNK!

An extra-big blast of fire shot out of its nose and a curtain of flames danced around its lips.

'Look, Borgon,' said Grizzy. 'Why don't I find some wood and get a little fire going, then you can make the toast on that? You can still tell everybody that you used a dragon.'

'Barbarians don't lie!' said Borgon crossly. 'And anyway, that dragon doesn't scare me.'

'Well, even if you don't care about yourself, what about that poor little slice of bread?' said Grizzy.

'The bread?' said Borgon.

'Yes, it wants to be a NICE piece of toast, not burnt to bits.'

Borgon stopped.

'Oh,' he said. 'I never thought of that.'

Grizzy quickly held out the triple-headed spear.

'Why don't you put the bread on the end of this?' she said.

'Then you can get away faster if things turn nasty.'

Borgon put the bread on the end of the spear, then very quietly crept up to the dragon. He made his way round it until he was facing its great head. The dragon's eyes were still closed and the flames were still flickering up from its nose. Borgon held out the spear at arm's length.

Soon there was a nice smell of toasting bread.

Borgon took a deep sniff. Lovely!

Grizzy took a deep sniff. Lovely!

Even the horses took a deep sniff. Lovely!

Then the dragon took a deep sniff. Lovely!

'Hurry up, bread,' muttered Borgon.
'You're nearly done!'

A long green tongue slipped out from between the dragon's lips, and snaked upwards to give the bread a big soggy lick.

'GET OFF!' shouted Borgon.

He snatched back the spear and accidentally whacked the dragon on the nose. The dragon's eyes snapped open and the great head reared up. Borgon turned and ran.

VAROOOOSH!

A blast of flame shot out and set fire to the back of his trousers.

'YEEOWWW!' screamed Borgon.

He ducked behind the cactus with smoke pouring up from his bottom. Luckily the dragon was too dazed to have seen where

he'd gone. It laid down its head and went back to sleep.

Grizzy took the spear from Borgon and inspected the bread. 'It's only done on one side,' she said. She pulled the bread off, turned it round and put it back on.

'Stand still,' said Grizzy, then she walked round behind Borgon.

'What ARE you doing?' demanded Borgon.

'Finishing the toast, of course,' said Grizzy, holding the bread over his rear end.

Borgon looked round and suddenly realised his bottom was on fire. 'ARGHHH!' The barbarian jumped around slapping out the flames with both hands.

'Oh, Borgon!' moaned Grizzy, looking at the piece of bread. 'You big soft dandy! It's hardly toasted at all. You might have waited a bit longer.'

Grizzy put down the spear then ran over to a strange little cactus she'd seen next to the horses. It was shaped like a green cross with a bright blue flower on the top. She poked her finger in through the side, then wiggled it around and pulled out a blodge of green pulp. She ran back and offered it to Borgon.

'What's that supposed to be?' asked Borgon.

'Rub it on your burn,' she said. 'Go on, do it!'

Borgon scooped the pulp from her finger and did as he was told. Slowly a smile came to his face.

'Ahhhhh, that's better!' he said. 'What IS that?'

Grizzy got out her book and showed him a picture.

'It's a Green Cross Cactus,' she said. 'It can mend wounds, cure headaches, stop nosebleeds and get rid of spots.'

'Nice!' said Borgon.

'But don't confuse it with the CROSS GREEN cactus,' said Grizzy, reading the book.

'It smells like a bonfire of old socks and shouts rude words if you whistle at it.'

'Ha ha ha!' they both laughed.

Grizzy closed the book. 'We'd better be getting home,' she said.

'Not yet!' said Borgon. 'This toast is only done on one side. I'm not going to have you telling everybody that a barbarian leaves a job half done.'

'Are you mad?' gasped Grizzy. 'The dragon's only dozing. It'll blast you as soon as it sees you.'

'Then I'll have to move fast,' said Borgon.

'And there's only one way to do that.'

Borgon took the triple-headed spear and lashed it to his horse so that it was sticking out backwards over the horse's tail. To make it longer, he tied the fork onto the spear, then he stuck the bread on the very end. The horse stopped nibbling the cactus he had found and looked round. He liked his new long tail. It was the longest tail in the Lost Desert, and it had a fork with a piece of bread on the end! That was nice.

Borgon climbed on to his horse and got ready to gallop right past the dragon's head. This was going to be GREAT! One good blast of flame would be enough to finish the toast, and then, as long as he got his timing right, he'd be well out of the way before his bottom caught fire again. Even mad Uncle Jing would have been impressed.

GRORNK!

The dragon opened one eye. Then the other. Its tail began to twitch and it tried to push itself up with its front legs.

'Quick Borgon,' said Grizzy. 'Before it gets moving!'

'**YARGHHHH!**' shouted Borgon and his horse surged forwards.

GALLOPY GALLOPY WHIZZ!

The dragon had just got to its feet as the bread flew past its nose. It gasped in a deep breath to make a mighty blast of fire, and at the same time it lashed out with its front leg. The dragon's long claws caught the very end of the spear and ripped off the bread.

'Borgon!' shouted Grizzy. 'The bread!'

Without thinking, Borgon looked round, and so did his horse, who saw the end of his long tail lying on the ground.

The next thing Borgon knew, his horse had spun round and was running back, straight towards the dragon. The head reared up and the giant mouth opened.

'WAH!' screamed Borgon, covering his face with his arms.

But then a stone flew through the air and smacked the dragon hard on the nose. The beast's head turned, the flame shot out, it missed Borgon and the horse and instead toasted a large rock off to the side. The dragon charged forwards, following the flame and bashed its head on the rock in a shower of sparks.

KAL-LACK-AR-ACK!
SPLORF!

The great beast ended up lying on its side. It was knocked out cold and all its flames had gone.

Borgon got down from his horse and took a few deep breaths to steady himself. He couldn't believe that Grizzy had managed to hit an attacking dragon right on the nose with a stone. If she'd missed, he would have been sizzled to bits. What a shot!

'Borgon, are you OK?' shouted Grizzy as she dashed towards him.

'No,' grunted Borgon. 'I'll never finish the toast now, and it's all your fault.'

Grizzy looked a bit upset, and Borgon felt

really mean. But what could he do? He was a barbarian! Barbarians couldn't go thanking normal savage girls for saving their lives. Of course not. So Grizzy would have to stay being upset and Borgon would have to stay feeling mean and that was all there was to it.

Borgon went to give the big dragon's head a gentle shove with his boot. When nothing happened, he pulled one of its giant eyelids open. The orange eyeball didn't even twitch.

'Why did the dragon run into that rock?' asked Grizzy.

'It's been a bit clumsy all along,' said Borgon. 'It was swaying about when it came flying from the Punch Pit.'

'The Punch Pit!' realised Grizzy. 'It must have drunk some of that smelly purple lake! No wonder it was all dizzy and confused.'

'How utterly useless,' said Borgon. 'I'll never get that slice of toast finished properly now.'

Borgon went to pick up the fork.

Gloop Glump Glurge! went the dragon's stomach.

'What's happening?' asked Borgon.

'Oh no!' said Grizzy. 'You know you what you said about your Uncle Jing blowing the backside off his trousers . . .'

Borgon saw the dragon's belly quiver and

tail twitch, then it let off a truly frightful stink right in his face.

'OO-URGHHHH!' coughed Borgon.

He dashed off, clutching his nose with both hands, and ended up dropping the fork. The handle stuck in the ground leaving the toast propped up in mid air. Borgon had barely got out of the way when a massive spout of flame shot out of the dragon's bottom, followed by a cloud of green smoke.

THRURRRRPPPP!

'YUK!' screamed Borgon and Grizzy.

Slowly the smoke and smell drifted away. Once again the dragon was lying motionless, and stuck on the end of the fork was . . .

'. . . one absolutely perfectly cooked slice of toast!' exclaimed Borgon.

A Little Thank You

The dragon had done its job perfectly. As it lay sleeping off the effects of the Punch Pit, Borgon picked up the fork. He tucked it into his belt, then went over to the dragon.

'Thanks for the Best Barbarian Breakfast Ever!' he said.

'Come on, Borgon,' said Grizzy. 'Let's go

before it wakes up.'

But then Borgon saw that the dragon's belly was still bleeding. 'I'm not leaving it like this,' he said. He wiped the worst of the blood away and checked on the wound.

'Ooh, nasty!' he said. 'It's deeper than I thought. Could that strange little cactus help?'

Grizzy opened her book. She found the right page, then went to dig down underneath the Green Cross cactus. She ripped out a clump of sticky root wool, then brought it back to Borgon who helped her pull it into a square shape. They plastered it over the dragon's wound, and left it there to do its magic. Soon the injury would heal and the great dragon would live on to have many more fantastic fights, and give other brave savages their own amazing stories to tell.

And that was how it should be.

Borgon and Grizzy got on their horses and headed back to Golgarth Basin. Borgon was full of the happiness that can only come when you've had a true barbarian adventure. The vultures still circled overhead, the snakes still hissed from under the cactus leaves and another old yak collapsed and died on the stone plains of the Lost Desert. It had been a perfect morning and it was just about to

get even better.

Welcome Home

Grizzy hadn't said a thing since they left the sleeping dragon, but finally she spoke.

'Borgon?' she said. 'You know how you picked up the dragon's trail from a piece of grass and two pebbles? I've got to tell you, that was totally amazing. I had no idea you could do stuff like that.'

Borgon tried to stay cool but he couldn't. Grizzy had just said EXACTLY what he'd wanted to hear. And before he could stop himself, he heard himself saying:

'I can't believe you managed to hit that dragon on the nose with a stone. You were so fast. I've never seen anything like it.'

The two looked at each other suspiciously. This 'being nice' thing was all a bit uncomfortable.

'It's just a pity you're so bad at everything else,' said Borgon.

'Are you kidding?' said Grizzy. 'I'll race you back.'

'Eat my dust!' shouted Borgon.

'YARGHHHH!'

The two of them shot off towards Golgarth Basin. They galloped between rocks, jumped over cactuses, and kicked

up great clouds of sand and tiny spiders. Although Grizzy's little grey horse had shot ahead to start with, Borgon's horse was bigger, stronger and far more used to riding

flat out across the desert, especially with a chubby boy on its back waving an axe and shouting '**YARGHHHH!**'.

Borgon was well ahead by the time he came around the last corner. In front of him was the gap in the rock wall that led into the basin, and inside he could see his mum's dark red horse tied up outside their cave. He couldn't wait to give Fulma her surprise!

He was just pulling up his horse when heavy footsteps came running towards him. It was Mungoid, and he was looking worried.

'Get away!' warned Mungoid. 'Go on, hide! Your mum's going mad about this dangerous breakfast.'

'But she's not meant to know,' said Borgon. 'Who told her?'

'Hunjah,' said Mungoid. 'She's got him trapped in your cave.'

'Never mind,' said Borgon. 'She's just worried about me, but I'm back now. She'll be fine.'

'Oh no she won't!' said Mungoid. 'I've heard her screaming. Now GO!'

Borgon tried to pull his horse round and gallop away, but the horse was feeling tired. It decided to fold its back legs and sit down, just like a dog. Borgon slid straight down the horse's back and landed on the rocky ground.

SLA-BUMP!

Borgon leapt to his feet, but before he could run off, a voice called him back.

'STAY THERE!'

Fulma stepped out of the cave.

'Oh mighty me,' whimpered Mungoid, then he hurried off to hide behind a rock.

Fulma's dark red hair was sticking right out like the spikes on a porcupine.

'Hello, lovely Mummy,' said Borgon. 'Did you have a nice time?'

'Don't you LOVELY MUMMY me!' snapped Fulma and she bared her teeth. Borgon had forgotten she'd just been to have them sharpened. My goodness, the teeth sharpener had done a very good job. They looked like two rows of white needles. Oo-er!

By this time Hunjah and Fulgut had

arrived too, along with Grizzy's mum, Gavista. It was obvious the two mums had been having a blazing row.

'What have you done with Grizzy?' demanded Gavista.

'Nothing!' said Borgon.

'Oh no?' said Gavista. 'You took her to get a dangerous breakfast.'

'Don't deny it, Borgon,' said Fulma. 'Hunjah told us.'

'Sorry, Borgon,' said Hunjah. His big hat was wobbling and his thin little knees were knocking. 'They made me tell them!'

Poor Hunjah. Borgon knew his friend would have tried to keep quiet, but nobody could hold out for long if Fulma was doing her freaky face.

'Don't listen to Hunjah, Mum!' said Borgon. 'He only eats tomatoes. He thinks everything else is dangerous.'

'That's not true,' said Hunjah. 'I like bananas too. And lettuce.'

'BE QUIET!' snapped Gavista. 'Where's Grizzy?'

'She's right behind me,' said Borgon. 'Look!'

They looked out of the gap in the rock wall, but all they could see was the empty path leading out across the Lost Desert. There was no sign

of the girl on the little grey horse. Gavista turned on Fulma.

'Your son went off to get a dangerous breakfast with Grizzy, and now he's come back alone. Your son has eaten my daughter! I know he has. You barbarians are all the same.'

'Fulgut!' demanded Fulma. 'Do you know anything about this dangerous breakfast?'

'Who? What? Me?' The big old barbarian looked a bit sheepish. 'Oh no. I'm sure it was just a harmless bit of fun . . .'

'Harmless fun?' screeched Grizzy's mum. 'LOOK AT HIM!'

They all looked at Borgon. The dragon's

blood on his clothes was drying and flaking off, he was battered and bruised, and the back of his trousers had been burnt away.

'Calm down, Mum,' said Borgon. 'I was making a nice surprise for you. Look!'

But when Borgon reached down to pull the toast from his belt, it had gone!

'Borgon!' hissed Fulma. 'Where's Grizzy? Tell us NOW.'

Borgon could feel his mother's eyes boring into him. His head was starting to throb, his teeth were scraping together, and he was feeling cold, very cold.

Borgon dragged his eyes away and looked round. There was still no sign of that awful girl! But then he spotted a scratch on a rock and some tiny scuff marks in the sand. Suddenly he knew where Grizzy was.

‘Mungoid!’ croaked Borgon. He managed to raise a finger and point out towards the desert.

Borgon’s chunky friend leaped up from behind his rock, then he charged over to the basin entrance and looked round the corner.

‘She’s here!’ shouted Mungoid. ‘She’s been hiding.’

Sure enough, Mungoid came back leading the grey horse with Grizzy on it. She was looking as well and as happy and as irritating as ever.

‘Hey, Borgon, you dropped this!’ laughed Grizzy, waving something. ‘Ha ha!’

‘What is it?’ gasped Gavista.

'It's what Borgon calls dangerous,' said Grizzy.

'But . . . but . . . it's only a slice of toast!' gasped Gavista.

'Hur hur hur!' laughed Fulgut quietly. 'Well done, son! Hur hur hur!'

Gavista was already backing away from Fulma, but too late. The tall, spiky-haired savage took a deep breath and then the words started firing from her mouth like hot darts.

'So! You think you can come round here INSULTING barbarians and then you have the NERVE to accuse my son of EATING your daughter when all the time they were just having a HARMLESS little ride with no danger to anyone . . .'

Fulma didn't stop talking until Gavista had scurried right across to the far side of the basin and hidden herself away in her cave. Grizzy tossed the toast over to Borgon then rode off to join her mum, but not before she'd given him a friendly wave. Of course Borgon and Grizzy were always going to be enemies, but they were going to be NICE enemies.

Borgon passed the toast over to Fulma.

'Here you are, Mum,' said Borgon. 'You told me to be more like Dad. Well, how about this?'

Fulma took it, then sniffed it, then bit off a tiny corner.

'By the gods!' she said. 'Is this what I think it is?'

Fulgut and Borgon both nodded.

Fulma's face broke into a huge beaming smile. 'Now that's what I call a real barbarian breakfast!'

The Last Sneeze

That night, Borgon was lying on his mammoth skin rug in the mouth of the cave. It had been a brilliant day and it wasn't just because of the dragons and the riding and the shouting '**YARGHHHH!**'. It was also because he'd had fun with Grizzy (although he would never admit it) and then he'd spent the whole afternoon and evening telling Mungoid and Hunjah about the dangerous breakfast. Every time he'd finished the story, they'd asked him to tell it all over again.

Each time Borgon told the story, the dragons got nastier, the fights got longer and a few times Borgon had even been frazzled and swallowed alive, at which point they would all roll around laughing and then Borgon would have to start all over again.

Borgon yawned a mighty barbarian yawn and took a final look around the dark basin. A few smoky lanterns were flickering outside caves, while higher up the moonlight was glinting off some silvery bones scattered along the rock wall. The vultures had settled into their messy nests and the rattlesnakes were all curled up under the cactuses like cosy little cupcakes. The Lost Desert had gone to bed.

And then, in the faraway distance, the baby dragon sneezed in his sleep and accidentally roasted a little bunch of flowers that had been left on a mushroom next to him.

KATCHOOSH!

But Borgon didn't hear it. He was already snoring his head off.